Includes compact disc.

For Mareen,
my younger sister
A.W.

For my kids,
Max and Chella
M.A.

Lola's Fandango

Barefoot Books
2067 Massachusetts Ave Cambridge, MA 02140

Text copyright © 2011 by Anna Witte
Illustrations copyright © 2011 by Micha Archer
The moral rights of Anna Witte and Micha Archer
have been asserted
Music by Brian Amador, Greñudo Music (BMI)
Narration by The Amador Family
Recorded and produced by Amador Bilingual Voiceovers,
Cambridge, MA
First published in the United States of America
by Barefoot Books, Inc in 2011 All rights reserved
Graphic design by Ryan Scheife, Mayfly Design,
Minneapolis, MN
Reproduction by B & P International, Hong Kong
Printed in China on 100% acid-free paper
by Printplus, Ltd
This book was typeset in Dalliance, Mrs Eaves and Kingdom
The illustrations were prepared in collage

ISBN 978-1-84686-174-1

Library of Congress Cataloging-in-Publication Data
is available under LCCN 2008028143

3 5 7 9 8 6 4 2

Lola's Fandango

Written by **Anna Witte** Illustrated by **Micha Archer** Narrated by **The Amador Family**

Barefoot Books
Step inside a story

Lola and her family live in a small apartment in a building
called The Park. The building is in the middle
of the city. There is no park. But there is traffic.
Honk hooonk go the cars.

Lola has one older sister.
Lola thinks her sister has the better name.
Cle-men-ti-na sounds so much better than *Lo-la.*
Clementina is taller than Lola. And her braid
is longer than Lola's arm.

"You have such beautiful hair," says Lola.
"When you're older, you'll have hair just
as beautiful," says Clementina.
Lola looks at herself in the mirror. Her hair is
coarse and wiry like a terrier.

Clementina paints very well. The other day she painted
a cat so perfect, it licked its paw when she was done.
"She's talented, our Clementina," says Papi.
Mami nods. Lola looks at her own painting.
Her camel looks like a whale.

Clementina has friends.
They wear pretty, ruffled dresses
and have ice cream in
the kitchen. Then they go into
Clementina's room and
close the door.

"Let me in," says Lola as she
knocks on the door.
"Not now," says Clementina.
    "When you're older, you'll
get your own room."
    "Not fair!" says Lola. She
hides in the closet in
Mami and Papi's bedroom.

The closet smells like Mami's
perfume. There are many boxes
    in the dark corners, behind
the long coats. Lola opens the
    first one. Winter clothes! *Pfew!*
They smell like mothballs!

Lola opens the second one. Letters, so many letters! Lola recognizes Abuelita's tiny handwriting. "Abuelita," she says, "I miss you."

The third box has a red lid with golden writing. It looks expensive. Lola lifts the lid carefully.

A pair of shoes! They have high heels and go *toc toc* on the wooden floor, *toc toc* through the hallway, *toc toc* into the kitchen. Mami is sitting at the sewing machine. The sewing machine goes *tictictictic…tictictictic*.

"Mami, why don't you ever wear these shoes?"

"Put those shoes back right where
you found them, Lola," says Mami.

"Those are shoes for dancing, not for walking."

"Dancing? What kind of dancing?" asks Lola.

"Flamenco," says Mami.

"Flamingo?"

"Flamenco. It's a Spanish dance."

"Does Clementina dance flamenco?" Lola asks.

"No," Mami answers. "Now put those shoes away."

"Papi," says Lola the next day. "What's
flamenco dancing like?"
"You should ask your mother about that. She used
to dance all the time," says Papi, twirling
his mustache.
"She won't tell me anything," says Lola.
"No? She was very good, you know.
Let me show you." Papi opens his wallet and
takes out a small photograph.

"That's Mami?" Lola's eyes get very big.
"She looks so different!"
In the photo, Mami wears a dress with ruffles
and polka dots. Her arms are up in the air.
"Can you dance flamenco too?" Lola asks.
"A little bit. Your mother and I used to
dance together sometimes." Papi smiles and
looks out the window.

"I want to learn," says Lola.
"You?" Papi raises his left eyebrow. "But it's difficult.
And you need *duende*."
"What's that?"
"Spirit. Attitude."

"But I have that!" Lola shouts and throws her
arms in the air and makes a serious face
like Mami in the picture. Papi laughs.

"Pleeeease!" says Lola. "I promise I'll practice a lot."
"All right, all right," says Papi. "I'll teach you."
"But don't tell Mami. Or Clementina," says Lola.
"It'll be our secret," says Papi.

That evening, when Mami and Clementina
go to the grocery store, Lola takes her first lesson.

"The most important thing in flamenco
is rhythm," says Papi. "Before you start
to dance, you have to be able to
clap the rhythm. Listen…"

1-2-3　4-5-6　7-8　9-10　11-12!

"All right?"
"All right," says Lola.
"Now let's clap together," says Papi.

1-2-3　4-5-6　7-8　9-10　11-12!

"Not bad," says Papi and smiles. "Now practice
this until you know it in your sleep."
"But I want to dance," says Lola.
"You will," says Papi. "In a few days.
Now it's time to go to bed."

Lola cannot fall asleep for a long time.

1-2-3   4-5-6   7-8   9-10   11-12!

The raindrops on the window sing:

1-2-3   4-5-6   7-8   9-10   11-12!

The clock on the wall ticks:

1-2-3   4-5-6   7-8   9-10   11-12!

The cars in the street honk:

1-2-3   4-5-6   7-8   9-10   11-12!

And then Clementina says,
"Wake up, Lola *dormilona!* Breakfast is ready!"

"I know it in my sleep! I know it in my sleep!"
says Lola. She runs to tell Papi.
"What do you know in your sleep?"
Clementina asks, but Lola is already out the door.

When Mami and
Clementina go to visit
Tía Clara a few days later,
Lola has her
next lesson.

"Today you will learn
to stomp your feet,"
says Papi.
"It goes like this."

Papi dances.
He makes a lot of noise.
Toca toca TICA!
Toca toca TICA!
And Lola dances.
Toca toca thump!
Toca toca thump!
Toca toca...
THUMP!

Lola falls to the ground.
"Waaaah!" she cries.
"Lola," says Papi,
"flamenco dancers
don't cry."

Lola stops crying.
No, flamenco dancers
do not cry.
She gets up again.

BAM! BAM! BAM!
The neighbor downstairs
knocks on the ceiling
and shouts, "Quiet up
there! What's all
this racket?"

"¡Ay!" says Papi. "We
need to find a different
place to practice."
"We can practice on the
roof," Lola suggests,
"where we hang our
laundry to dry."

"Great idea.
Nobody will bother
us there. We'll go there
tomorrow. Don't forget
to practice."

And Lola practices.

She brushes her teeth:
Toca toca TICA!

She combs her hair:
Toca toca TICA!

She makes her bed:
Toca toca TICA!

On her way to the market
with Mami, her
feet dance:
Toca toca TICA!
Toca toca TICA!

Mami gives her a
funny look, but she
does not say anything.

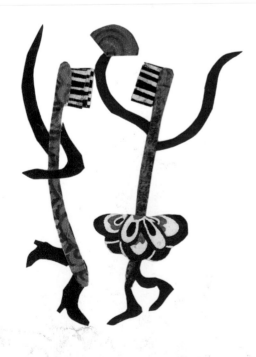

"It's nice outside," says Papi the next evening.
"Lola and I are going out for a walk."

But they don't go for a walk. They go up
to the roof. There is plenty of room to dance
among the clotheslines and there are
only pigeons to watch them.

"Tonight," says Papi, "you will learn how to
move your arms and hands. Watch me. Lift
your arms in the air, round and graceful,
and turn your wrists."
"Like this?" Lola asks, turning her arms like windmills.
"Just your wrists," says Papi. "Your hands
should move like the wings of birds."
Lola watches the birds. Lola watches Papi.
And Lola dances.

She snaps her fingers: *Snap! Snap!*
Spring carries flower petals through the air.
She taps her heels: *Tap! Tap!*
Summer clouds dot the blue sky.
She whirls her skirt: *Swish!*
Fall blows leaves and raindrops across the roof.
She stomps her feet: *Toca toca TICA!*
Soon it will be too cold to dance on the roof.

One day Papi says, "It's Mami's birthday soon.
Let's organize a surprise party for her."
"Can I dance?" Lola asks.
"Yes, I hope you will," says Papi.
Suddenly Lola is worried.

"But I don't have a dress," she says.
"The one you are wearing is fine," says Papi.
"It doesn't have any dots," Lola protests.
"You don't need polka dots to be a
flamenco dancer," says Papi.
But Lola is not convinced.

Papi, Lola and Clementina prepare
Mami's surprise party. Papi invites all their friends,
and they fill the small apartment with
laughter and food and guitars. There are so
many people, there's no room for them to hide.

When Mami comes home and opens the door,
they all scream, "Surprise!"
Everyone gives Mami a hug. "Oh! Oh!" says Mami.
But she smiles.

"Come here, Lola," says Papi. "It's time for
you to show Mami your surprise."
"NO!" says Lola, and she runs out
of the party and into her room.

Papi follows her.
"What's wrong, my little Lola?" he asks.
"I can't dance in front of all those people!"
says Lola. A big tear rolls down her cheek.

"I just can't — I don't even have a dress."
"But you have *duende*, Lola. You told me all those
months ago, remember? Having *duende*
means having the courage to dance away your fear."

Lola nods. She wipes away her tears.
"Maybe this will help as well," says Papi,
and he hands Lola a box with a big red bow.

"For me?" Lola asks. "But it's Mami's birthday."

Papi smiles. "Just open it."

Lola opens the box and takes out a beautiful ruffled dress.

"It's got polka dots!" she cries. She shivers all over

and gives Papi a big hug. "Thank you," she whispers.

"Wait. There's more," says Papi,

pointing at the box.

Nestled in red tissue paper is a pair

of dancing shoes, with little silver nails

in their heels.

"Oh!" is all Lola can say.

She puts on her new dress. It fits perfectly.

She puts on the shoes: *Toca toca TICA!*

They dance across the floor toward the mirror.

"I'm a flamenco dancer," Lola whispers.

Then she twirls into the living room.

"*¡Ole!*" shouts Tía Clara, and Tío Carlos

strums a few chords on his guitar.

Papi starts to clap:

1-2-3 4-5-6 7-8 9-10 11-12!

Soon everybody is clapping:

1-2-3 4-5-6 7-8 9-10 11-12!

Papi lifts Lola onto the kitchen table.

"*¡Que baile! ¡Que baile!* Let her dance!"

And Lola snaps her fingers: *Snap! Snap!*

She taps her heels: *Tap! Tap!*

She whirls her skirt: *Swish!*

She opens her fan: *Zum!*

Then she stomps her feet: *Toca toca TICA!*

And the table bounces: *Toca toca TICA!*

The dishes clink: *Toca toca TICA!*

The windows rattle: *Toca toca TICA!*

And the walls shake: *Toca toca TICA!*

Everyone is cheering.

"Bravo, Lola! *¡Así se baila!* That's how it's done!"

Mami smiles at Lola.

"Gracias, mi niña," she says. "Thank you."

Then she gets up on the table to dance as well.

Toca toca TICA!

Toca toca TICA!

Toca TICA!

Toca TICA!

Toca TICA —

BAM! BAM! BAM! The neighbor downstairs
knocks on the ceiling. Tía Clara slips out to invite
him to the party.

"¡Ole!" shouts Lola.

"¡Ole! ¡Ole!"

THE FANDANGO

Flamenco is a style of traditional Spanish dance known for colorful costumes, powerful movements and lots of hand clapping and rhythmic foot percussion. It is an energetic and exciting dance. In this book, Lola learns a twelve-beat flamenco rhythm with the emphasis on the third, sixth, eighth, tenth, and twelfth beats. *Fandango* is one of many flamenco rhythms, and it is also the traditional name for an informal gathering or fiesta where song and dance are performed.

GLOSSARY

These are the Spanish words used in Lola's story:

Abuelita—*Grandma*

dormilona—*sleepyhead*

duende—*spirit/attitude*

Gracias, mi niña—*Thank you, my girl*

Mami—*Mama/Mom*

¡Ole!—*verbal encouragement among flamenco performers*
The stress is on the *o*, not on the *e*. "Olé" with an accent is of French origin.

Papi—*Papa/Dad*

¡Que baile!—*May she dance! Let her dance!*

Tía—*Aunt*

Tío—*Uncle*

Barefoot Books
step inside a story

At Barefoot Books, we celebrate art and story that opens the hearts
and minds of children from all walks of life, focusing on themes that
encourage independence of spirit, enthusiasm for learning and respect
for the world's diversity. The welfare of our children is dependent on
the welfare of the planet, so we source paper from sustainably managed
forests and constantly strive to reduce our environmental impact.
Playful, beautiful and created to last a lifetime, our products combine
the best of the present with the best of the past to educate our
children as the caretakers of tomorrow.

www.barefootbooks.com

Anna Witte

was born in Germany and brought up in Madrid, Spain. She finds inspiration for her stories in the European and Central American cultures she knows so well. She first brought her signature style to Barefoot Books in *The Parrot Tico Tango*. Anna lives with her husband in Washington State where she teaches Spanish and Latin American letters at the University of Washington.

Micha Archer

grew up painting alongside her mother, who is a watercolor artist. Micha worked for many years as a kindergarten teacher before venturing into illustration. Her favorite media to work with are gouache, watercolor, pen and ink, and collage. Micha has also illustrated Barefoot Books' *The Wise Fool*. She and her husband divide their time between western Massachusetts and Costa Rica.

The Amador Family

Rosi and Brian, along with their twin 15-year-old daughters, Sonia and Alisa, are Latin musicians whose voices and original music bring *Lola's Fandango* to life. Rosi and Brian have toured the world since 1984 with their Latin band, *Sol y Canto,* and other groups, and also work as voiceover actors. They live a musical life in Cambridge, Massachusetts.